Can You Hear Me Smiling?

A Child Grieves a Sister

By Aariane R. Jackson

Illustrated by Leigh Lawhon

Child & Family Press

Washington, DC

Child & Family Press is an imprint of the Child Welfare League of America. The Child Welfare League of America is the nation's oldest and largest membership-based child welfare organization. We are committed to engaging people everywhere in promoting the well-being of children, youth, and their families, and protecting every child from harm. All proceeds from the sale of this book benefit CWLA's programs in behalf of children and families.

CHILD WELFARE LEAGUE OF AMERICA, INC.
HEADQUARTERS
440 First Street, NW, Third Floor, Washington, DC 20001-2085
E-mail: books@cwla.org
Website: www.cwla.org

Material on p. 25 quoted from *Lifetimes: The Beautiful Way to Explain Death to Children,* by Bryan Mellonie and Robert Ingpen (Bantam Books, 1983). Reprinted by permission.

CURRENT PRINTING (last digit)
10 9 8 7 6 5 4 3 2 1

Cover design and text design by Amy Alick Perich
Edited by Tegan A. Culler

Printed in the United States of America

ISBN # 0-87868-835-8

Library of Congress Cataloging-in-Publication Data

Jackson, Aariane R.
  Can you hear me smiling? : a child grieves a sister / by Aariane R.
Jackson ; illustrated by Leigh Lawhon.
      p. cm.
  ISBN 0-87868-835-8 (alk. paper)
  1. Bereavement--Psychological aspects--Juvenile literature. 2. Brothers
and sisters--Death--Psychological aspects--Juvenile literature. I. Lawhon,
Leigh. II. Title.
  BF575.G7J28 2004
  155.9'37'083--dc22
                         2004000531

This book is dedicated to
my beloved sister, Alaunda (Londee),
and to my loving mother,
who has inspired me throughout my life.

Preface
by Arnelle Jackson

When my 9-year-old daughter Aariane faced the worst time of her life, I felt painfully incompetent. As parents, we try to battle our children's fevers and colds. We soothe their cuts and bruises. From broken toys to broken hearts, we endeavor to mend the pieces of their lives. In unconditionally loving, protecting, and defending our children, we offer generous advice and solace. We try, but we can't always protect them from pain, or prepare them for every contingency—certainly not for the devastation of losing a sibling.

The death of Aariane's older sister Londee hit harder than an earthquake. The two of them had been inseparable, and now that special person in her life was gone. To make matters worse, six weeks after the tragedy, Aariane suffered the trials of being a third grader in a new school. On her own all day, without her sister and her old friends, she began to dislike school. Her honor roll status dropped to below average. I noticed dramatic changes in her behavior, as well as in her eating and sleeping habits. She grew lethargic, sullen, and distant. She was afraid of being alone. How terribly she missed her sister, she confided. Why did people have to die?

I was at a loss and felt quite helpless. How could I comfort her through this tidal wave of pain and sorrow? My frustration was compounded by my own sorrow and affliction, my own grieving process. Aariane needed outside help, and fast. It shouldn't be difficult to find—or so I thought.

I had succeeded in finding information and books written exclusively for grieving parents. To my amazement and distress, the literature for young grieving children was almost nonexistent! Hopeful leads on the subject yielded too little information to be of any long-term value. I kept checking, thinking that perhaps books for children would surface soon.

They didn't.

Meanwhile, Aariane and I turned to Scriptures. Our studies gained momentum. One book, *Lifetimes: The Beautiful Way to Explain Death to Children,* by Bryan Mellonie and Robert Ingpen (Bantam Books, 1983), was especially useful; it is this book to which Aariane refers in her narrative. That book, however, did not focus specifically on some of the unique issues Aariane faced in losing her older sister. She decided that she wanted to help other children understand their feelings after the death of a sibling. Together, we sat down and discussed the idea of writing. The catharsis began with her first written word.

As one courageous survivor, Aariane remembers the fun she had with her sister, and the heartbreak of losing her best friend. She states that children cannot actually prepare for the death of a sibling. But if it happens, it's important to know that there are other young survivors who have been through the experience, and who care. Aariane encourages love and respect for brothers and sisters even when it seems impossible, but her story also makes clear that there was nothing she did to cause her sister's death, and nothing she could have done to prevent it. As normal children, she and Londee had fights, but Aariane knows that those fights did not lead to Londee's tragic death.

Aariane shows that it is possible to move on. Admittedly, it's not easy. Praying for strength, talking to adults, and spending time with friends all help in the recovery. Most importantly, memories never die. Aariane's older sister will always live on in her heart and in her soul.

Big sisters. Who needs them? They are always doing things to little sisters, like making us laugh, then making us cry. They stick out their tongues at us for no reason, and pull our hair when no one is looking. Londee poured bubbles in the bath water after I told her not to. I remember our last bath together, and the mean thing I said to her.

I was sitting in the tub of water minding my own business, when she climbed in with me, grabbed the bubble bath, and started pouring.

"Stop it!" I screamed. "No bubbles!"

But Londee wouldn't stop. In fact, she laughed at me. The bubbles got higher and higher. I tried to kick every one of them to her end of the tub.

"Don't you want to have fun?" she asked me, still pouring.

"No, I don't. No bubbles."

"It won't hurt you."

"If you don't stop, I'll tell Mommy," I yelled.

"No you won't," she giggled.

Londee loved to tease me at bathtime. We were too big to fit in the tub together, but we did it anyway, maybe to get on each other's nerves.

Sometimes I liked her bubble people and the bubble beards she put on my face. But not tonight. I didn't feel like bubble people and bubble beards. And worse, she wouldn't stop laughing at me. The kids at school used to laugh at me, too. They made fun of my long feet, and how tall I was for my age.

All of a sudden, I felt mad and mean. I looked for something to throw at her—a toy boat, soap, anything to make her stop. I splashed water as hard as I could. Bubbles popped in my nose and eyes and hair. They stung.

That did it. Now I was really, really angry. Then I said the mean thing: "I don't like you, and you're not my real sister anyway."

I didn't know that Londee would wake up sick the next morning and eventually go to the hospital. It didn't occur to me to apologize to her when she first got sick. Kids get fevers, and they usually aren't a big deal. I didn't know that for seven weeks, I would wait for her to come home, but that she would never come home again. During those seven weeks, I would make plans: First, I thought, I'll tell her I'm sorry for the mean thing I said. Then we'll play dolls and bake mud cookies in our backyard oven. I'll be nicer when we take baths together. If she wants bubbles, I'll let her have bubbles. Bubbles won't hurt me, I told myself.

I didn't know that when I would see her for the last time in the hospital and finally tell her how sorry I was, it would be too late. If she heard me, she didn't answer. She was too sick by then.

Meanwhile, when she first got sick, I was happy to be her little nurse. I sang to her and changed the TV channels. I fed her soups and juices, and fixed ice packs for her hot forehead. I knew she liked my attention, even though she said she didn't. I was the expert. I knew everything about Londee, even the two pills she'd been taking every day of her life. Whatever the doctors needed to know about my sister, they could ask me.

But they never did. They had their own ideas. "Pneumonia," the doctors had said. It sounded to me like "ammonia."

Finally, Londee's breathing got worse, and the doctors said she had to go to the children's hospital across town. Mommy and I went with her and stayed until very late. It was around midnight when we got ready to go home. "Aren't you afraid to stay here by yourself?" I asked her.

"Leave me alone." She wiggled her nose. "I'm asleep."

I stared at her face for a long time. She had the fluffiest cheeks and the cutest little nose. Her eyebrows were dark and smooth. I listened to her breathing, in and out, in and out. I thought for a minute, should I? She wouldn't like it, but I decided I was going to do it anyway. I kissed her on the cheek. There. It felt good to tease her for a change. "Night-night, Londee. I'll see you in the morning."

It was my first night alone in our bedroom. There was nobody to giggle with me under the covers, nobody to toss me stuffed animals, nobody to say "Stop playing and go to sleep." I tried turning my face to the wall, so that I wouldn't have to see Londee's empty bed. But that didn't work either, because my mind knew that her bed was empty.

We had never been apart before. Her adoption had been a year before mine, and from the beginning, we always did everything together. We rode bikes together, we played dolls together. We ate off each other's plates. We both loved pizza and fried chicken and hated sweet potatoes and beets. We slept in the same bed until I was seven. I could count on Londee to tell me what to do and say. She didn't mind if I wore her coats, dresses, and slips, but never her shoes. Londee wanted only her feet in her shoes. I loved how she fixed my hair, real fancy, with pretty ribbons and barrettes. She pinched the mean kids at school who wouldn't leave me alone. Except at bathtimes, Londee was my best friend in the whole world. I knew—well, I thought—that we would be together forever and ever.

The next morning, Mommy and I were up early. She was getting dressed to go to the hospital. I faked a smile when she pushed me off to school. I thought I shouldn't have to go, but she said, oh, yes, I did. I told her I would go by myself.

"I'm nine years old. It's just down the street, and there's only one little street to cross. I'm not afraid to walk by myself," I said, which wasn't the truth.

I stood at the curb of the little street. The weather was warm, but my body felt cold. I should have told Mommy the truth, I thought, looking back at our house. Londee is the brave one. She always looks out for cars and for strangers who might kidnap little kids. "You can do this," I said to myself. "Take your time. Remember to look both ways, and behind you. Ready, set—go!" I gave my body a big push and kept my feet moving, half running, half skipping all the way to school. I couldn't wait to tell Londee what I'd done. Now I was brave too.

A few mornings later, Londee got sicker. Mommy rushed to the hospital to be with her all day. Our cousin—we called her "aunt" because she was a grownup in her forties, just like Mommy—picked me up after school and took me home with her. Mommy came home late, looking very tired. Our phone rang and rang. Mommy talked to everyone but me. I felt left out and tired. Londee is my sister, I thought. I'm not too young to understand things. If she needs surgery, I know all about surgeries. I've seen plenty of them on TV. The doctor operates, and pretty soon the patient gets well again. I'm not too young to understand things.

I looked around for something to do. I wandered back to our bedroom and poked around the toy chest. Most toys just weren't any fun without Londee. I picked up our babydolls. It wouldn't take me very long to get them cleaned up. They hadn't been playing much lately, so they weren't very dirty.

"Let's do something fun," I said to them. "What about skating? No? A picnic at the beach? What's wrong? Why won't you move your arms and legs?" I felt sorry for them. They missed Londee and her action adventures—safaris, scuba diving, mountain climbing—things I didn't know how to do. Then I said, "How about a true story? We'll call it 'The Londee Story.'"

"I first saw Londee when she came with Mommy to my foster home," I told the dolls. "I was three years younger, and almost her size. She smiled at me a lot and acted very friendly. I'd never seen a person make such ugly, funny faces." I tried to show those faces to the dolls. "I liked her right off. I could tell that she liked me too. One day, I went home with my new family for good. And we lived happily ever after. Did you like the story?" I looked down beside me. The babydolls were asleep. I covered them up, and then we took a long nap.

One morning, I heard Mommy talking on the phone. "Is this the gift shop? Yesterday, I saw a huge stuffed palomino horse. Yes, that's the one. Please hold it for me. I'm on my way to the hospital."

A giant horse? Probably another gift for Londee, I thought, feeling left out again. She already has enough flowers and toys and balloons. Sick people get everything. When I get sick next time, I thought, I'm going to ask for a giant horse, or a giant something.

Mommy named the horse Samantha. She was the most beautiful horse I'd ever seen, real or fake. Her mane and tail were long, fluffy, and snow-white. She had big, happy brown eyes, and a huge red bow around her neck. I rubbed her tummy. She liked that. When I kissed her nose, she wiggled in my arms. Squeezing her felt like squeezing a real person. Samantha was bigger than big. I could hardly carry her. "Be careful not to muss her bow," the clerk said to me.

In the elevator, I hugged Samantha tight, wanting her to be mine. She loves me and I love her. If I promise to take good care of her, if I promise not to ask for anything else, maybe… .

We walked through the double doors. Something's wrong, I thought right away. Asking Mommy for Samantha would have to wait.

Londee's old room was empty. We found her in another room down the hall. "Wait here," Mommy told Samantha and me at the door. I sneaked up close and peeked inside.

The room was full of doctors and nurses. They were busy with machines and tubes. There's Londee in bed. Is she breathing? Yes, she's breathing. What's wrong, then? I wondered. One doctor looked up and saw Mommy. I tried to read his lips, but people kept moving and getting in the way. Mommy signed some papers, then rushed out of the room. "Hurry, I'll explain in the car," she said. I had to run to keep up with her.

"Your sister is very sick and has to go to a university hospital two hundred miles away," Mommy said. "They have a special respirator—a machine that helps her breathe. After we get home, we'll pack our suitcases. You'll be staying with your aunt and uncle. A helicopter is coming soon for Londee."

A helicopter? No fair, I thought. "Are you going to fly with her?" I asked.

"There won't be room for me," said Mommy. "I'll have to drive."

Then Mommy started to cry. Seeing her cry scared me. Londee must be sicker than I thought. Why can't I go with them? I'll be good. I won't get in the way. Without them, who will tell me what to wear, when to eat, and what time to go to bed? I didn't get to tell Londee goodbye. Before Mommy left, she kissed my cheeks and ears and neck. I waited until later that night to cry.

There's no place like home. I missed everything about our house. I missed its smell. I even missed our furniture. It was late when Auntie and Uncle went to bed. Their house was very dark. I lay awake, listening to the spooky sounds in the other rooms.

"Samantha?" I whispered, glad that Mommy had let me keep her. "Londee has to be home by this Sunday." Samantha asked me why. "Because, silly, it's Easter. She can't miss our egg hunt in the backyard. We'll have eggs dyed in all colors, marshmallow chicks, and all kinds of jellybeans. I'll give you your own basket, and whatever you find, you get to keep. You'll love it. Just wait and see."

Mommy called Saturday night. The egg hunt for tomorrow was off. "Londee is too sick, and we won't be coming home," she said.

Too sick? What did that mean? I didn't want to think about it. "Auntie gave me an Easter basket," I told her. "I'll save Londee some candy." Or try to, I thought. I'd almost eaten the treats down to the artificial grass. "When can I come visit her?"

"Soon, real soon."

"Good, because I have a new ugly face to show her, even uglier than hers. I stick my thumbs in my ears, wiggle my fingers, cross my eyes, and push my tongue way up inside my top lip." This was the funniest and ugliest face of all faces. Londee would laugh so hard, she'd forget the mean thing I said to her.

I spent a lot of time talking to Londee in that lonely bedroom, while I was hugging Samantha.

"Today we had a tornado drill at school. The teachers made us sit down in the hall and put books over our heads. You should've seen me. I couldn't keep my knees pulled up to my chest. Remember those brown shoes? My feet kept sliding because they're so slippery on the bottom. What? Yes, everybody at school asks about you. Your girlfriends and the principal stop me in the halls all the time."

I couldn't tell her this part, though: I liked it when the teachers who used to hug her hugged me instead. If I was out sick, would they miss me so much? Maybe not. Londee and I were very different.

Londee loved school. I could take it or leave it. Londee always kept a neat bookbag. Mine was held together by safety pins. Londee loved to read. Reading gave me a headache. Londee was short with meat on her bones. I was tall and skinny. We both had long hair, but hers was thicker and easier to curl. Londee wanted to meet her birthfamily someday. Not me. I had Mommy and I had her, and that was enough for me. Being different from each other didn't matter. We were still best friends.

Mommy took me to visit Londee three times after she was moved to the university hospital. There was a platform beside her bed. I climbed up and held on to the railing. The last time I came, Londee's eyes were closed. She looked pretty to me, like one of our babydolls.

"Talk to her," Mommy said, "She can hear you."

"Hi. It's me." I tried to smile as I talked. Could Londee hear that, too? "Kids at school sent you more cards. See? They miss you, and I do too." I talked on and on. Talking kept me from crying. I wished that she could talk back to me, wished that she could come home.

Mommy touched my arm. "It's time for me to go," I told her. "Oh, I'm sorry for saying you're not my real sister, because you are."

I gave Londee a kiss goodbye, for the last time.

My sister passed away on a Saturday, the exact date of her adoption seven years before. It was almost as if she had died on her birthday, or on a special anniversary. Mommy came home early. She sat me down on the sofa, put her arm around me, and told me. Things around me started spinning, faster and faster. I couldn't see. My hands and feet felt cold, and I was crying. My stomach hurt, deep, deep down inside. It's not true, I thought, crying harder. Londee is asleep in the hospital. Her lungs need more time to get better. She'll be coming home soon. She knows how much I need her.

But it was true. Londee was gone from us. She had been too sick, and couldn't get well again.

It seemed right to do what I did next. Londee's babydolls were sitting on her bed. I lined them up, the little ones in front, then fed them, dressed them, and combed their hair. I knew that she would have done the same for me.

Our house was quiet now. I missed the sounds of singing and laughing. My days were sad and lonely because my sister had gone from us. Even when I wasn't crying, the sad feeling inside me wouldn't go away.

Adults tried to help. "God knew best and called Londee to be one of His little angels," they said. But angels lived in heaven, and heaven was a place too far for me to go. I knew what had happened. But why? Why did my sister pass away?

One day, I found the answer all by myself.

I saw the light on in Mommy's room. She was sitting on her bed, reading from a little black Bible. Her face was long and sad like mine. I sat down beside her, then opened one of my books. The social worker at the hospital had sent it to me. Inside were color pictures of plants and animals and people. I read out loud, "There is a beginning and an ending for everything that is alive. In between is living." Every living thing had its own lifetime. If the living thing got too sick or injured, it could die because it couldn't get well again. A very sad thought, but it made some sense to me. "Londee's lifetime was twelve years," I said.

Now, whenever I feel sad, I read to Mommy. "Sometimes, living things become ill or they get hurt. Mostly, of course, they get better again…"

But I know that sometimes they don't. That's the end of their lifetime. And when that happens, the people around them miss them. I found out that feeling sad is okay after losing someone you love.

Londee's lifetime was twelve years. Half of her years were spent being my big sister and having fun.

I dream good dreams of her many nights, and always wake up feeling very tired. She is a cute brown rabbit with fluffy cheeks and a wiggly nose. She is a pretty butterfly. I can see her smile on its wings. She is a busy, busy little ant.

Her adventures are as real as they ever were. I can hardly keep up with her.

About the Author

Aariane R. Jackson wrote *Can You Hear Me Smiling?* in 1996, when she was 9 years old. She will graduate from high school in 2005, and hopes to pursue a career in writing and law.

Jackson Family, 1990

Clockwise from top: Arnelle,

Aariane, and Alaunda (Londee).

For Parents, Professionals, and Other Caring Adults

by J. Scott Hinkle, PhD, and Ann S. White, LPC, CT

In our twenty years as children's counselors and grief specialists, we have learned that all significant losses affect children, but the shattering effect of a sibling's illness and death changes the life and perspective of a child forever. A child who loses a sibling faces all the pain and sorrow that any death causes, plus a host of additional issues that are specific to the death of a sibling.

The aftermath of a child's illness and death can feel like an extended earthquake to the entire family, and especially to the surviving children. Nothing is in its place, and everyone is trembling and feeling the aftershock. It's difficult to find safety—all the people involved are in danger of having things fall down on them. People whom a child once thought of as "strong" are now crying out in new ways and struggling for their own survival. Often they become unavailable to provide support for other family members, including the surviving children. What was once stable has become shaky and terrifying.

A child who has lost a sibling has lost a lifetime companion, playmate, rival, and confidant. A complicating factor is that the child must often struggle with an entirely different kind of loss—the loss of his or her parents to grief. Children look to their parents for guidance and comfort in new and painful situations. Unfortunately, many adults in our culture have not been taught to grieve in healthy ways. Some rush to suppress painful memories and stifle painful discussions. Others become obsessed with the deceased child, ignoring the needs of surviving children. And even the healthiest, most well-adjusted parent must cope with his or her own grief, anguish, and sense of loss. It is difficult to shepherd others through the grieving process while you are going through it yourself.

Outsiders—friends, clergy, and professional counselors—can be of enormous help. They can step in to fill the gap until parents have regrouped their strength and clarity and are ready to function as sources of support and comfort to their children.

Children face an array of issues following the illness and death of a sibling. After all, during normal times, the relationship between siblings can be difficult. It is expected that brothers and sisters will engage in some competition, fighting, and jealousy. Children often wish that siblings would vanish so that they can enjoy their parents' undivided attention, have their own room, or not have to babysit the "bratty little tagalong" or be bossed around by the mean older brother. It is not uncommon for children to think this way or even hurl such sentiments at each other. "You should never have been born!" "I wish you were dead!" "Go away and never come back!" And then, horrifyingly, their wish seems to be "granted" when the offending sibling actually dies.

The guilt that follows can be devastating. Very young children, who still engage in magical thinking, often believe that they have actually caused the sibling's death. And even older children, who have presumably outgrown this mode of thinking, still feel guilt. Sometimes the surviving child may remember only the unpleasant times, and

may feel bad to have caused the deceased to suffer during his or her lifetime. Some families unwittingly reinforce this belief by thinking of the dead child as the "good one" and glossing over all faults or difficulties the child had caused during his or her life. The remaining child then takes on the role of the "bad one." He can never compete with his dead sibling's memory. Even normal reprimands are taken as a sign that he is a "wrongdoer" compared with the now-perfect and sainted deceased sibling. Many children we have worked with have regarded themselves in this light and believe that their parents wish they were dead, instead of their sibling. In fact, Judith Guest's well-known book *Ordinary People,* which was made into a movie in 1980, deals with a young boy who reacts in exactly this way to the death of his older brother.

Guilt can be the result, too, of resentful feelings the child may have experienced during the sibling's illness. A sick youngster who has received a great deal of attention, gifts and visits from distant relatives, and a "vacation" from school may incite jealousy in the other siblings, who are expected to carry on with life as "normal" when nothing is normal. Children may feel guilty about ordinary worries (a fight with a friend, a run-in with a teacher, not making the baseball team) because these concerns are "trivial" next to the life-and-death illness of the sibling. After the death, they may feel shy about bringing up these "petty" issues to their grieving parents. And they may feel guiltiest about the mere fact that they survived while their sibling didn't make it. Survivor's guilt—"Why didn't God take me instead of her?"—is common among people of all ages who have lost loved ones, but especially among children whose brother or sister has died.

Children who have lost siblings may also lose friends. Other children may start to avoid them, or may become excessively meddlesome. Peers may treat them differently, or just not understand what they are going through. Some younger children may be shunned by schoolmates who think that whatever killed the sibling is contagious. Older children and teens may turn to unsavory companions who offer new distractions, or to drugs and alcohol.

They may also reevaluate their religious beliefs. Even young children who hear well-intentioned folks say "God took your sister" may express anger at God, or fear that God will likewise take them. Older children may formulate their concern in a more sophisticated way, asking the age-old question of why the innocent suffer and the wicked prosper. The reassessment of religious beliefs that were once secure is part of the broader, often overwhelming turmoil with which a child who has lost a sibling must deal.

What to Look Out For

Grieving children often experience physical symptoms, such as exhaustion, headaches, stomachaches, bedwetting, and difficulty with weight control (excessive weight loss or weight gain). They may have psychological symptoms, such as confusion, withdrawal, fear of being alone, fear of going to sleep (some children see sleep as being similar to death), and fear of death—especially when they reach the age at which the brother or sister died.

Of course, each child will react differently. Some children will talk about their feelings; others will be unable to express themselves verbally. This may be because they are too young to have the vocabulary necessary to articulate their pain, or because they are disinclined to use speech as a medium of self-expression. Some children will become angry, others weepy, and others may appear "stony" and indifferent. This is why it's important to be alert to signs of grief and to learn how to handle them.

What to Do

It is important to give your child as many choices as possible. This will give your child a sense of control at a time when everything seems to have spun completely out of control. Allow him to attend the funeral if he wants to. Respect his decision without pressure or disapproval if he decides not to. The same holds true for viewing the body, visiting the grave, or attending memorial services. Initially, it may be helpful to keep visits from strangers and acquaintances to a minimum; bereaved children need to be close to their family and a few others. Later, it is helpful to reach out to specific outsiders for support and help. These may include professional counselors, relatives, school personnel, church officials or members, neighbors, friends, coaches, youth leaders, or a local hospice organization if it provides services for youngsters. See if you can find a grief support group for children in your child's age group.

Don't suspend your household rules and routines, even during the initial grieving process. Children obtain security from daily routine. On the other hand, don't be afraid to bend the rules when necessary. A "mental health" day away from school might be very healing. If your child decides that tonight she is finally ready to visit the grave, don't say, "Homework comes first." Be sensible in walking the two extremes of rigidly enforcing rules and routines, and completely abandoning them. Provide structure with room for flexibility.

Allow your children to deal with their grief in their own way. Provide plenty of play supplies that might serve as media of expression, such as markers and crayons for drawing and clay that can be used for pounding or shaping. Some children will find it therapeutic to be outdoors and engage in physical activity. Others may prefer to play music, pound nails, dance, or sing. Like Aariane, many children may find that writing can lead to healing.

Always reassure your child that he or she is loved and protected. Make sure she understands that she was not responsible for the sibling's death, and that you are happy she is still alive. Don't compare her to her deceased sibling ("Your sister always kept her room neat…"), because these types of comparisons can increase feelings of guilt. Always remember to be a good listener. Try to read the message underneath your child's words, and listen for the needs and meanings that she may not be able to articulate yet. And accept whatever she does say, even if it seems shocking or different from what you expected. There are no right or wrong feelings at a time like this, and your child needs your companionship and validation more than ever.

It is our hope that Aariane's book will provide an important medium that you and your child can use to open up discussion and to help your child feel less alone. Like a support group, *Can You Hear Me Smiling?* can help children understand that their reactions are normal and that they, too, can heal.

We all need to remember that the loss of a loved one teaches us what and who is most important in our lives. It provides us with an opportunity to live differently. Living the experience of loss and grieving presents us with an unasked-for gift, wrapped in an excruciating package. Each of us must explore and uncover what that gift is. Aariane can teach all of us what it feels like to be a bereaved child, and how our grief can be transcended and healed.

J. Scott Hinkle, PhD, a licensed psychologist and a nationally certified counselor, is currently the Clinical Training Administrator for the National Board for Certified Counselors in Greensboro, North Carolina. He is the author of *Promoting Optimum Mental Health Through Counseling* (1999) and the coauthor (with Michael E. Wells) of *Family Counseling in the Schools* (1995). Dr. Hinkle has a private counseling practice in Greensboro, North Carolina.

Ann Sparling White, LPC, CT, has been helping children, parents, educators and health professionals better understand and support human reactions to grief and loss for 25 years. Presently, she is employed with Hospice and Palliative Care of Greensboro, North Carolina, as a Family and Children's counselor in the Kids Path Program. A nationally certified counselor, she also works with the Guilford County, North Carolina, schools as a grief consultant and has developed children's bereavement groups, a nationally recognized puppet presentation for elementary students, and camps for bereaved children. She also maintains a private counseling practice where she works with loss issues other than those resulting from illness and death.

Leigh Lawhon (illustrator) is a graphic designer and illustrator in Washington, D.C. *Can You Hear Me Smiling?* is her first children's picture book.